NoGGiN
and the Storks

For Cillian, Kiera,
Poppy and Lilya

EGMONT

We bring stories to life

First published in Great Britain 1973.
This edition first published in Great Britain 2017 by Egmont UK Limited
The Yellow Building, 1 Nicholas Road, London W11 4AN
www.egmont.co.uk

Text copyright © The Estate of Oliver Postgate 1973
Illustrations copyright © Peter Firmin 1973
The moral rights of the illustrator have been asserted.

ISBN 978 1 4052 8144 7

A CIP catalogue record for this title is available from the British Library.

Stay safe online.
Egmont is not responsible for content hosted by third parties.

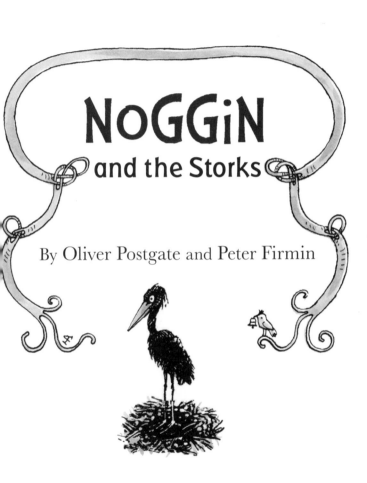

NoGGiN
and the Storks

By Oliver Postgate and Peter Firmin

EGMONT

This is the castle of Noggin the Nog.
Noggin the Nog lived here a long time ago.

This is the little town beside the castle
of Noggin the Nog.

This is where the Nogs live
in little houses with straw roofs
and stone chimneys.

Sometimes, in the springtime,
tall birds with black shaggy feathers
would come and make nests
on the Nogs' chimneys.
They were called sooty storks.

9

Sooty storks liked to make nests on chimneys, because the smoke kept their eggs warm.

The Nogs did not like the nests on their chimneys, because the smoke from their cooking fires would not go up the chimneys.

The smoke got in their eyes.

The smoke made them cough.

The Nogs were not friends
with the sooty storks.

One year there were more sooty
storks than usual.

The Nogs asked them to go away.
The storks did not go away.

The Nogs pulled twigs from their nests.
The storks brought more twigs.

The Nogs picked up stones to throw at the
storks, but Thor Nogson told them not to.

He said, "Noggin would not like you to hurt the birds."

Then the angry Nogs marched into
Noggin's castle.
They marched up to Noggin.
They said, "The storks have blocked our
chimneys. Our houses are full of smoke.
Let us chase the storks away."

Noggin was worried.

He did not want to hurt the storks.

The Nogs said, "Let us throw stones at them.

Let us chase them away."

Noggin was worried.

He did not know what to do.

Then a small brown bird flew in.
It perched on Noggin's helmet.
It carried a little bell.
It rang the little bell.

Noggin said, "Small brown bird,
why do you ring a little bell?"
The bird did not answer, but Nooka answered.
She said, "The bird is reminding you
that you are king of the birds
as well as king of the people."

Then Noggin knew what to do.
He said, "When we have found a place
where the storks can lay their eggs and
keep them warm, we will send them there.
Until then, they can stay on the chimneys."

Then Noggin called for his inventor.
He said, "Send for Olaf the Lofty.
Olaf the Lofty is a clever inventor,
Olaf the Lofty will think of something."

Noggin told Olaf the Lofty to think of
a place where the storks could
make their nests and keep warm.
Olaf the Lofty said, "I will think.
I will think of a place where the storks
can make their nests and keep warm."

Olaf sat on the wall and thought.
Olaf thought and thought,
but he could not think of anywhere
that was warm enough for storks
who liked to live on chimneys.

Then the small brown bird came and
rang her bell.

Olaf held out his hand.
The small bird perched on his hand.
Olaf said, "Shall I follow you, bird?"
The bird nodded and flew away,
ringing her bell.

Olaf followed the small brown bird.

The bird led him to this place.
This place is an old chalk quarry.

Around the edge of the quarry
were six old hollow oak trees.

It was not a nice place, but the small
brown bird flew round and round and
rang her bell as loudly as she could.

Olaf the Lofty was puzzled.
He did not know why the bird
had chosen this place.
Olaf the Lofty thought and thought.
Olaf the Lofty was a clever inventor.

He suddenly saw why the bird
had chosen this place.
He jumped up and ran to the town.

He shouted, "Bring iron sheets and pipes
and logs and iron bars!"
The Nogs ran to help him.

They carried the things to the chalk quarry and helped Olaf with his work.

This is what they made.
They made a big fireplace with six chimneys.
The six chimneys led to the six hollow oak trees.
When they lit the fire, the smoke went up
inside the oak trees.

The storks were delighted.
They helped the Nogs carry their nests
to the chalk quarry and fix them
in the oak trees.

43

The storks lived there all summer.
They were black with soot, but happy,
and their eggs were warm.
The Nogs kept the fire going under the nests
and fed the storks because they were friends.

In the summer the sooty eggs hatched.
When the autumn came the Nogs helped
to teach the young sooty storks to fly.

Then, one day, all the storks flew away.
"Goodbye!" shouted the Nogs.
"Come again next year!"

The end